Party Time, Poppy!

1806

Look out for other
LITTLE DOLPHIN titles:

Hattie's New House
Milo's Big Mistake
Oscar's Best Friends
Fergal's Flippers
Sammy's Secret

And if you've enjoyed reading about
Little Dolphin and his adventures,
why not try reading the Little Animal Ark
books, also by Lucy Daniels?

Party Time, Poppy!

Illustrated by DAVID MELLING

LUCY DANIELS

Hodder Children's Books

A division of Hodder Headline Limited

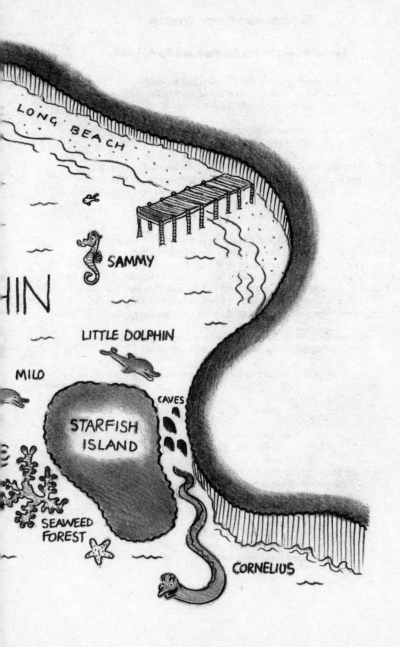

To Alexandra Poppy Westrop

Special thanks to Jan Burchett and Sara Vogler

Text copyright © 2004 Working Partners Limited
Created by Working Partners Limited, London, W6 0QT
Illustrations copyright © 2004 David Melling

First published in Great Britain in 2004
by Hodder Children's Books

3 5 7 9 10 8 6 4 2

A Catalogue record for this book is available from the
British Library

ISBN 0 340 87347 7

Printed and bound in Great Britain by
Clays Ltd, St Ives plc

The paper and board used in this paperback by Hodder Children's
Books are natural recyclable products made from wood grown in
sustainable forests. The manufacturing processes conform to the
environmental regulations of the country of origin.

Hodder Children's Books
A division of Hodder Headline Limited
338 Euston Road, London NW1 3BH

CHAPTER ONE

Little Dolphin was looking for
Poppy the spinner dolphin. His
best friend Milo was helping.
First, Little Dolphin checked behind
the rocks. Then he looked through
the pink fingers of coral growing
out of the reef. "Poppy's not here,
Milo!" he whistled.

There was a gush of bubbles
and Milo burst out from a kelp bush.

He shook the floppy leaves off his flippers. "She's not in there either," he chirped. "I've searched it top to bottom."

"Good," Little Dolphin said. "If she's nowhere near, we can make our plans in secret!"

It was Poppy's birthday tomorrow. Little Dolphin and Milo had decided to have a surprise party for her. All her friends knew they must keep it a secret from Poppy. But Poppy was the nosiest creature in Urchin Bay! It was hard to keep secrets from her.

Milo was full of bright ideas for the party. "We could ask the

seagulls to fly over and make
the word 'Poppy' in the air," he
suggested.

"What? Those silly gulls?"
Little Dolphin gave his friend a
playful nudge with his tail. "You
know they can't spell."

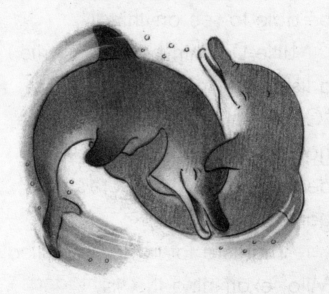

"I've got another idea,"

squeaked Milo. "Squids can squirt ink. We could ask Sid Squid and his friends to dye the bay in rainbow colours."

"But squids can only make black ink!" Little Dolphin whistled. "If the water turns black we won't be able to see anything!"

Little Dolphin began to write a list in the sand with his nose. "Come on," he clicked. "We've got loads more than the decorations to do. There's food, games, music ..."

"That is a lot to do," whistled Milo, examining the list.

"We could ask our friends to

help," Little Dolphin suggested.

"Good idea!" chirped Milo. "We'll go and see—"

"Hi there!" came a voice.

It was Poppy! She was spinning towards them with a determined look on her face.

Little Dolphin wriggled in the sand to get rid of the party list. Milo flapped his tail to help.

"I was wondering where you two were," clicked Poppy. "Anyone would think you'd been hiding from me." She stared at them. "What are you doing?"

"It's ... um ... a new dance," Little Dolphin squeaked as he wriggled.

"It's called the Squiddly Squid," added Milo, swinging his flippers too. "Have a go!"

"I don't feel like dancing," said Poppy sadly. "It's my birthday tomorrow and no one's remembered. I reminded Oscar just now but he shrugged his tentacles and swam off."

"But we'll all see you tomorrow, Poppy," Milo told her happily. "We're going to—"

"Wish you a happy birthday!" Little Dolphin interrupted, giving his forgetful friend a nudge with his nose.

"I should hope so!" snorted Poppy. "Well, can't stop now. I'm off for a nose round the bay. Coming?"

"Sorry, Poppy," Little Dolphin said. "We can't."

Poppy looked disappointed.

"But tell you what, we'll come surfing this afternoon," he added, before she could ask any awkward questions.

"All right," grinned Poppy. "See you then." And she swam away.

"Phew!" said Milo. "That was close!"

"And we still have so much to do," Little Dolphin whistled. "Let's ask our friends to help."

Oscar, Fergal the turtle and Hattie the hermit crab were

delighted to help with the party.

Hattie waved her claws for silence. "We could have the party at the old wrecked ship!" she clacked.

Everyone agreed that was a great idea.

"And I'll do the decorations," Hattie added.

"I'll help," said Milo.

"I can do the cake," said Oscar

the octopus. "And I'll be the waiter."

"No juggling with the plates though!" Hattie said bossily. Juggling was one of Oscar's party tricks but, when he did it, something always went wrong!

"I'll help with the cake and food too," said Milo.

"Music," whispered Fergal, nearly disappearing into his shell with embarrassment. Fergal was a very shy turtle, even with his friends. "I know someone to ask," he added, blushing.

"Who is it?" Little Dolphin asked.

But Fergal wouldn't tell. "You'll see," he murmured.

"I'll keep Poppy busy in the morning until everything is ready," Little Dolphin said.

"I'll help," said Milo. Milo wanted to help with everything!

"You'll be too busy helping everyone else, Milo," Little Dolphin told him. "But I will need a signal that the party is ready."

"Right!" squeaked Milo happily. Suddenly he jumped backwards on his tail and waggled his head as if a jellyfish had stung him.

"Are you all right?" asked Oscar.

"Yes," chirped Milo. "I'm showing Little Dolphin the signal!"

"So that's everything," said Hattie, clicking her pincers happily. Oscar clapped and Fergal gave his tail a shy wiggle.

But Little Dolphin didn't join in. He was thinking hard. Was there something else? Then he remembered. "We've forgotten one very important thing!" he squeaked.

Everyone stopped and looked at him.

"Presents for Poppy!"

CHAPTER TWO

The five friends looked at each other. Nobody had thought about presents!

"What do you think Poppy would like?" asked Milo.

"Claw mittens," began Fergal, then turned pink and pulled his head inside his shell. "Silly me!" came a quavery voice. "Poppy hasn't got claws."

"Nice idea though, Fergal," Little Dolphin said.

"I'd get her a glass necklace," clacked Hattie, "if I had enough limpets and barnacles to buy it with."

"And I'd buy juggling balls!" said Oscar, tossing some pebbles above his head. They landed on Milo's nose.

"Poppy can't juggle!" clacked Hattie.

"Neither can Oscar!" snorted Milo, rubbing his nose with his flipper.

"What about a shell bag or a coral flute?" Little Dolphin suggested.

Hattie shook her head. "None of us can afford to buy something like that."

The friends slumped miserably on the sea-bed. What could they do?

Then Fergal's little voice piped up from inside his shell. "We could buy one big present," he said, "if we put all our limpets and barnacles together."

"Brilliant, Fergal!" Little Dolphin exclaimed.

Fergal's shell wriggled with embarrassment.

The five friends put their limpets and barnacles in a pile and Hattie counted them. "Eight limpets and fifteen barnacles," she announced happily.

"Milo and I will go shopping later," Little Dolphin said. "We'll get something really nice for Poppy with all that!"

After lunch, Little Dolphin went to

call for Milo. He carried the
limpets and barnacles in a bag.

Milo rushed out of his cave to
meet him, swinging something
from his flipper. It was a gleaming
yo-yo made from two polished
shells. "My auntie brought this
back for me from Starfish Cove!"

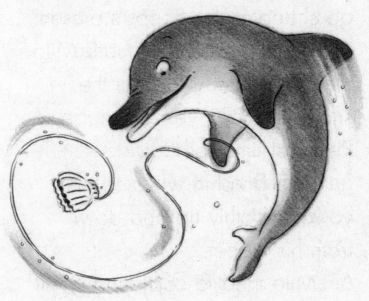

he clicked excitedly. "It's just like yours, Little Dolphin! But I'm having a bit of trouble. Mum won't let me practise indoors any more after I broke her best vase and clonked her on the head."

"I'll show you how to yo-yo," Little Dolphin offered. "Then we'll go shopping for Poppy's present."

"Poppy's present?" said Milo. He'd forgotten all about the shopping. "Oh yes, of course. Plenty of time for that!"

Little Dolphin whizzed the yo-yo smoothly up and down from his flipper.

Milo tried to copy and got it

caught in a nearby clam. "I'll try
again!" he chirped, as Little
Dolphin said sorry to the clam.
The yo-yo flew off into a clump of
sea cucumbers. "Hey, where's it
gone?"

"You're
supposed to
keep hold
of the
string!" Little Dolphin grinned.

All of a sudden something
spun into Little Dolphin and Milo,
knocking them sideways.

It was Poppy – and she looked
cross. "I've been waiting ages for
you two!" she whistled angrily.

Oh no! Little Dolphin and Milo were meant to be surfing with her – but they couldn't go now. They had to shop for her present!

Then Poppy saw Milo pick something up. "What have you got there?" she asked nosily, forgetting to be cross. "Wow!" she whistled. She was looking longingly at the yo-yo.

"I wish I had one! I must be the only dolphin in Urchin Bay without a yo-yo." She gave a sigh. "Come on, let's go surfing."

"Sorry, Poppy," Little Dolphin said, feeling very mean. "I promise I'll go with you tomorrow morning. But we can't go now. We've got … important things to do."

"Important things to do?" snorted Poppy. "Like playing with yo-yos, I suppose. See you tomorrow then – if you're not too busy." She stuck her nose up and swam off.

"Poor Poppy!" Little Dolphin clicked. "No one to play with and no yo-yo. But we'll make it up to her tomorrow." Suddenly he gave a happy chirrup.

"At least now we know the perfect present for her – a yo-yo of her own! And I know just the shop to find one."

Hidden Treasure was a dark, mysterious shop, full of lovely things to buy. Two snooty-looking seahorses were examining the displays. They looked down their

noses at Little Dolphin and Milo as the two friends swam into the shop.

An old catfish padded slowly across the cave floor on his feathery fins. His long black whiskers waved in front of him. It was Mr Cuthbert, the owner of Hidden Treasure. "Can I help you?" he asked.

"We've come to buy a yo-yo," Little Dolphin squeaked.

"A yo-yo," repeated Mr Cuthbert slowly. "Very popular item. I had a queue from here to the jetty this morning and everyone wanted a yo-yo. Rushed off my fins, I was."

"Can we see some, please?" Little Dolphin asked.

"It's to be a special present," squeaked Milo, "for our friend."

Mr Cuthbert poked around under the counter and pulled out a small wooden box. He nosed it open. "How about this?" Inside was a shiny yo-yo made of two black oyster shells.

"It's a Triton Tornado!" clicked Milo, jiggling with excitement. "Best yo-yo ever made! Poppy will love it!"

"How much is it?" Little Dolphin asked anxiously.

"Let me see," said Mr Cuthbert,

putting on a pair of glasses and squinting at the box. "Fifteen barnacles and ... nine limpets."

"Oh no," Little Dolphin groaned. "We have fifteen barnacles, but we're one limpet short!"

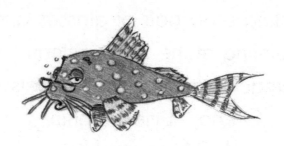

CHAPTER THREE

The two friends turned sadly
towards the door.

"Wait a minute," called Mr
Cuthbert. "Perhaps I can help."

Little Dolphin and Milo darted
eagerly back to the counter.

"As it's a special present, I'll
give you a special discount,"
said Mr Cuthbert. "You can
have the Triton Tornado for fifteen

barnacles and eight limpets."

"Thank you!" Little Dolphin and Milo exclaimed together, as Mr Cuthbert tied a piece of pink ribbon-grass round the box. "Poppy will be delighted!"

The next morning, Little Dolphin woke up extra early. He gulped down a quick breakfast and set off for Poppy's cave. He'd take her surfing while the others got the party ready. Milo would give him the signal when they were finished. He couldn't wait!

"Hello, Little Dolphin," said Poppy's mum as he swam up

to her cave. "Poppy said you were coming – but you're rather early. She's still in bed!"

"I was too excited to sleep, Mrs Whirlpool!" Little Dolphin squealed. "Poppy doesn't know anything about the party, does she?"

"Not a thing!" said Mrs Whirlpool. "She thinks everyone's forgotten her birthday! But surfing will cheer her up, I'm sure. I'll go and wake her."

Mrs Whirlpool came back looking very worried. "Poppy's not in her bedroom!" she wailed. "I can't find her anywhere!"

"She's probably waiting for me at the shore," Little Dolphin said.

"I don't think so!" sobbed Mrs Whirlpool. "She's taken her suitcase. She's run away!" Poppy's mum spun round the cave, flippers flapping wildly. "What are we going to do?"

"Don't worry, Mrs Whirlpool," Little Dolphin said quickly.

"She can't have gone far. I'll find her."

"Thank you, Little Dolphin!" said Mrs Whirlpool, slumping on to a rock. "I'll stay here, just in case she comes back home."

Little Dolphin swam off as fast as he could. Poor Poppy! Where could she be?

CHAPTER FOUR

Little Dolphin swam up and down
the reef looking for Poppy. He
searched the shallows near the
shore. This was one of her
favourite nosing places. But there
was no sign of her.

He looked out at the open
sea beyond Lighthouse Rock.
He felt a shiver of fear run up
his spine. Surely Poppy wouldn't

leave Urchin Bay on her own,
would she?

Little Dolphin swam towards
Lighthouse Rock. As he got
nearer he could see a queue
of sea creatures waiting for the
Whale Express. He remembered
when he and his dad had taken
the Whale Express all the
way to Puffin Island to see his
grandma. He'd loved the journey
in the little wooden cabin on

the whale's back. But would
Poppy dare to go on the whale
by herself?

He swam along the queue.
There was a family of seals at the
front and behind them old Mrs
Periwinkle gossiping to Mr
Hawkfish. Then there was a group
of little herrings chattering with
their teacher. The whole queue
looked happy to be going on the
Whale Express. All except one.

At the very end was a sad little figure with a suitcase. It was Poppy!

Little Dolphin darted towards her. "Poppy!" he whistled with relief. "I've found you!"

"Oh, it's you, Little Dolphin," said Poppy gloomily.

"Your mum's really worried," Little Dolphin said. "Why have you run away?"

"Because it's my birthday," clicked Poppy, "and no one's remembered."

"Your friends have remembered!" Little Dolphin whistled, putting a flipper round her. "Come back with me and you'll see."

But before Poppy could answer, somebody barged in between them.

"Morning, Poppy!" said a smooth voice. It was Vinnie, the shiftiest shark in Urchin Bay. He gave Poppy a toothy grin.

Little Dolphin knew that grin. Vinnie had something to sell, and it was sure to be a trick.

"Look what I've got for you!"
Vinnie held out a shiny yo-yo to
Poppy.

"Oh! Thanks,
Vinnie!" squeaked
Poppy. She glared
at Little Dolphin.
"At least *someone's*
remembered my
birthday!"

"It's not a present!" gulped
Vinnie, his eyes popping with
horror at the thought of giving
something away. "But as it's your
birthday, I'll do a swap. You
have this expensive yo-yo and I'll
have your old shell suitcase.

Can't say fairer than that."

Poppy looked longingly at the yo-yo. "Can I try it out?" she asked.

"No need," said Vinnie hastily. "Trust me, you won't find a yo-yo like it in any shop. Handmade! Lovely bit of workmanship."

Poppy held out her suitcase, ready to swap.

Little Dolphin didn't know what to do. If only he could tell Poppy about the Triton Tornado. He had to act fast. "Go away, Vinnie!" he said desperately.

"Why?" asked Vinnie, puzzled.

"I'm just about to close a great deal here!"

"Er ... your cave's on fire!" Only Vinnie could fall for something as silly as that, Little Dolphin thought.

"Blithering barracudas!" exclaimed the horrified shark. "My lovely cave!" He swam off in a panic, dropping the yo-yo.

The yo-yo sank down on to the sea-bed – and fell apart.

Little Dolphin had a closer look at it. It wasn't a proper yo-yo at all. Just two old bottle tops held together with a rusty nail.

Poppy nosed at the pieces that lay in the sand and burst into tears. "This is my worst birthday ever!"

"Never mind, Poppy," Little Dolphin said kindly. "Let's go and tell your mum you're safe and then we'll go surfing. You will have fun today. I promise!" Little Dolphin thought of Poppy's party with a tingle of excitement.

Poppy managed a small grin. "I'd like that!" she said.

The two friends sped off towards the reef.

As they went they could hear Vinnie's voice in the distance.

"Wait a minute! My cave can't be on fire. It's under water."

CHAPTER FIVE

"Whee!" cried Poppy as a foaming wave took her speeding along. "This is fun!"

Poppy had gone home, given her mum a big hug and promised never to run away again. Now she and Little Dolphin were surfing the Urchin Bay breakers while Little Dolphin waited for Milo's secret signal.

The two dolphins chased up and down in the rolling surf, chattering excitedly and catching the best waves to ride.

Suddenly, Poppy stopped and poked her nose above the water. "Look at Milo!" she giggled. "What *is* he doing?"

In the distance Milo was jumping backwards on his tail and waggling his head as if a jellyfish had stung him. It was the signal. The party was ready!

"Let's see what he's up to," Little Dolphin suggested. He knew Poppy wouldn't be able to resist being nosy.

"Good idea," clicked Poppy. "I was wondering where everyone was. Urchin Bay's never usually this quiet."

They skimmed out towards the middle of the bay. But Milo had vanished.

"He'll be hiding somewhere ready to jump out on us," Little Dolphin grinned. "Let's surprise him instead!"

"Yippee!" exclaimed Poppy, spinning with excitement.

"I love hide and seek."

Little Dolphin led Poppy down towards the sea-bed, darting behind rocks and bushes as they went. So far, everything was going to plan. But he didn't want Poppy to see the wreck until the very last minute.

They came to a huge clump of orange cup coral. The wreck was just on the other side. "I bet Milo is hiding behind there," Little Dolphin whispered. "You go first, and surprise him."

Poppy dashed round the coral – and stopped in astonishment!

The old wreck had been completely transformed. The tattered rope rigging was lit by glowing lantern fish. The broken deck was smothered in beautiful sea lettuces and eelgrass. HAPPY BIRTHDAY, POPPY! was written in the sand in brightly coloured seaweed.

"Who's done all this?" squealed Poppy.

There was a loud cheer and all Poppy's friends and family burst out from their hiding places. Poppy spun herself dizzy with delight.

Suddenly there was a roll of drums. Everyone looked towards the wreck. On the cabin were four grinning sharks with microphones. Fergal was standing shyly next to them.

"It's the Sharky Sharks!" shrieked Poppy. "I love them!"

The Sharky Sharks launched into their latest hit.

"Well done, Fergal!" Little Dolphin exclaimed. "When you said you'd sort out the music, I never dreamt you'd be inviting the most famous band in Urchin Bay!"

"They live next to my grandma," whispered Fergal. "I've known them since I was hatched."

"Let's party!" shouted Oscar, jiggling his tentacles in time to the beat.

The party was fantastic. Everyone danced round the wreck to the wonderful music. Then they played Sardines and Hunt the Kipper until Oscar called them all over.

"I hope you're all hungry," he said, balancing plates of seaweed sandwiches on his tentacles. He juggled the sandwiches above his head and skilfully tossed them to the guests. "I've been practising!" he said with a wink at Hattie.

When everyone had finished,
Hattie clicked her claws for
silence. "Time for the birthday
cake!" she called. She looked
round. "Where is it, Milo?"

"I hid it!" said Milo proudly.

"Where?" Little Dolphin
asked.

"Er … sorry," squeaked Milo.
"I can't remember!"

"You are a scatterbrain!" chuckled Hattie, tapping him with a pincer.

"It's Hunt the Cake time!" called Oscar. "Whoever finds it gets the first slice!"

Everyone jostled and giggled as the search for the cake began.

"I've found it!" squeaked Poppy at last.

She pulled the cake out from behind the rusty old cannon that stood on the deck of the wreck.

Little Dolphin grinned. He should have known that Poppy, the nosiest dolphin in Urchin Bay, would find it!

"Delicious!" said Poppy as she took a huge bite.

"Birthday cake?" said a voice. "Then I'm just in time!" It was Vinnie.

No one had invited the shifty shark – but that never stopped Vinnie, especially when he could smell food!

Vinnie barged through the

crowd just as Oscar the octopus was showing everyone his latest trick – spinning eight yo-yos at once.

"Help!" yelled Vinnie as eight yo-yo strings wrapped themselves around him. He was completely trapped. "Get 'em off me! Before the cake runs out!"

"I can't!" said Oscar. "The strings have all knotted."

"Useless things!" snapped Vinnie, wriggling helplessly. "You should have bought your yo-yos from me."

"I did!" chuckled Oscar, and everyone laughed.

There was a clash of cymbals and a beaming Poppy appeared on the deck.

"This has been a wonderful party," she said. "Thank you, everybody!"

"It was Little Dolphin and Milo's idea," said Hattie.

"But everyone helped," Little Dolphin insisted.

"And it's not over yet!"

 chirped Milo. He nudged Fergal forward.

Fergal made his way shyly towards Poppy with the wooden giftbox on his back. The other friends followed and gathered round as Poppy carefully untied the pink ribbon-grass. She nosed open the box. When she saw the Triton Tornado inside, she simply stared at it with her mouth open.

"Don't you like it?" Little Dolphin asked anxiously.

"We could take it back," added Milo.

"Don't you dare!" exclaimed Poppy. "It's perfect. It's the best yo-yo in Urchin Bay!"

Poppy took the Triton Tornado and spun it round her head. Then, as the Sharky Sharks started their next song, she suddenly began to wriggle in the sand, her tail flapping wildly.

Everyone watched in surprise.

"Are you OK, Poppy?" Little Dolphin asked.

"Too much cake," said Milo.

"Silly boys!" squeaked Poppy, swinging her flippers. "I'm doing the Squiddly Squid! You remember. It's the latest dance.

You showed it to me."

"Of course we did!" Little Dolphin laughed. "Come on, everybody! Get wriggling!"

Soon everyone was dancing the Squiddly Squid – even the Sharky Sharks!

LITTLE DOLPHIN: PARTY TIME, POPPY!

Now that you've finished this book, would you like another one to read, absolutely FREE?*

Your opinions matter! We've put together some simple questions to help us make our books for you better. Fill in this form (or a photocopy of it), send it back to us, and we'll post you another book, completely free, to thank you for your time!

Was this book …
( ) Bought for you ( ) Bought by you ( ) Borrowed for you
( ) Borrowed by you

What made you choose it? (tick no more than two boxes)
( ) cover ( ) author ( ) recommendation ( ) the blurb
( ) the price ( ) don't know

Would you recommend it to anyone else?
( ) yes ( ) no

Did you think the cover picture gave you a good idea of what the story would be like?
( ) yes ( ) no

Did you think the cover blurb gave you a good idea of what the story would be like?
( ) yes ( ) no

Please tick up to three boxes to show the most important things that help you choose books:
( ) cover ( ) blurb ( ) author you've heard of
( ) recommendation by school/teacher/librarian/friend
(please delete the ones that don't apply) ( ) advert
( ) quotes on the front cover from well-known people

( ) special price offer ( ) being a prize-winning book
( ) being a best-seller

Which of the following kinds of story do you like most?
(tick up to three boxes)
( ) funny stories ( ) animal stories ( ) other worlds
( ) people like you ( ) people with special powers
( ) scary stories ( ) stories based on a TV series or film

How old are you?
( ) 5–6 ( ) 7–8 ( ) 9–11 ( ) 12–14 ( ) 15+

Name
Address

Please get a parent or guardian to sign this form for you if you are under 12 years old – otherwise we won't be able to send you your free book!

Signature of parent/guardian_____
Name in block capitals_____ Date_____

*Offer limited to one per person, per private household. All free books worth a minimum of £3.99. Please allow 28 days for delivery. We will only use your address to send you your free book and guarantee not to send you any further marketing or adverts, or pass your address on to any other company.

Please send this form to:
Reader Opinions, Hodder Children's Books, 338 Euston Road, London NW1 3BH.
Or e-mail us at: readeropinions@hodder.co.uk if you are over 12 years old.